This Little Tiger
book belongs to:

_____

_____

_____

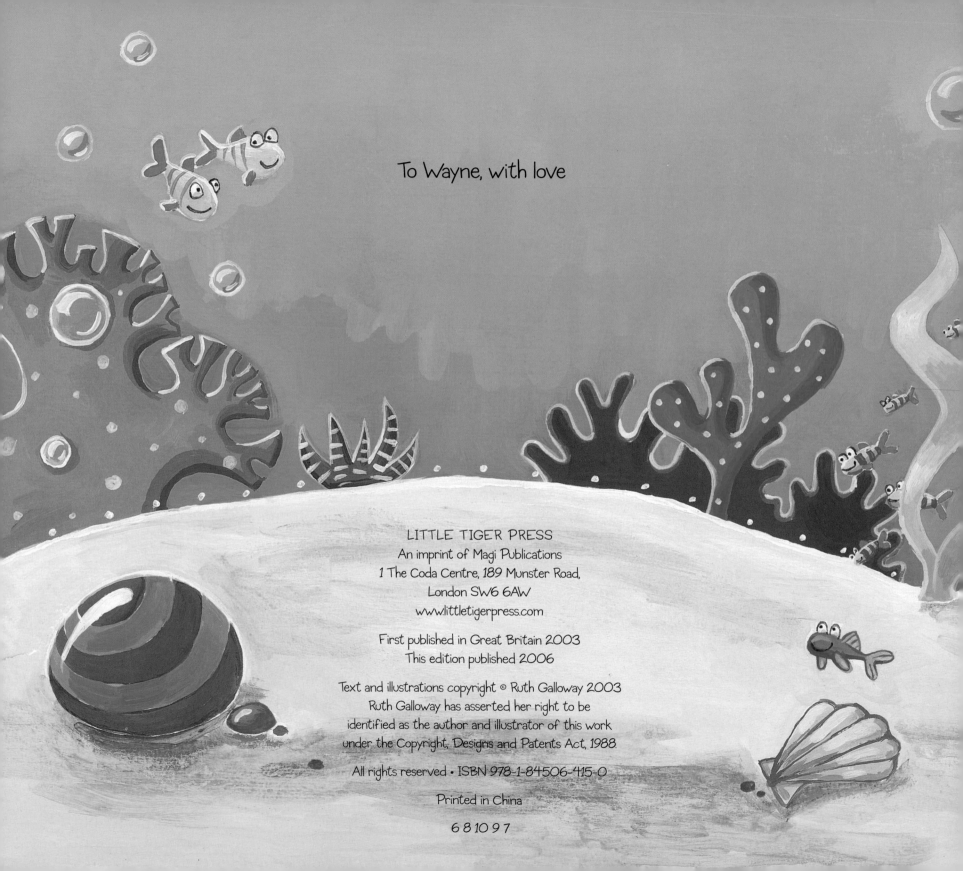

To Wayne, with love

LITTLE TIGER PRESS
An imprint of Magi Publications
1 The Coda Centre, 189 Munster Road,
London SW6 6AW
www.littletigerpress.com

First published in Great Britain 2003
This edition published 2006

Printed in China

6 8 10 9 7

Smiley Shark

Ruth Galloway

LITTLE TIGER PRESS
London

Far away, in a deep rolling ocean, lived Smiley Shark . . .
the smiliest and sunniest, the friendliest and funniest,
the biggest and toothiest of all the fish.

Every day Smiley Shark watched the beautiful fish
that dipped and dived and jiggled and jived,
and darted and dashed with a splosh and a splash.

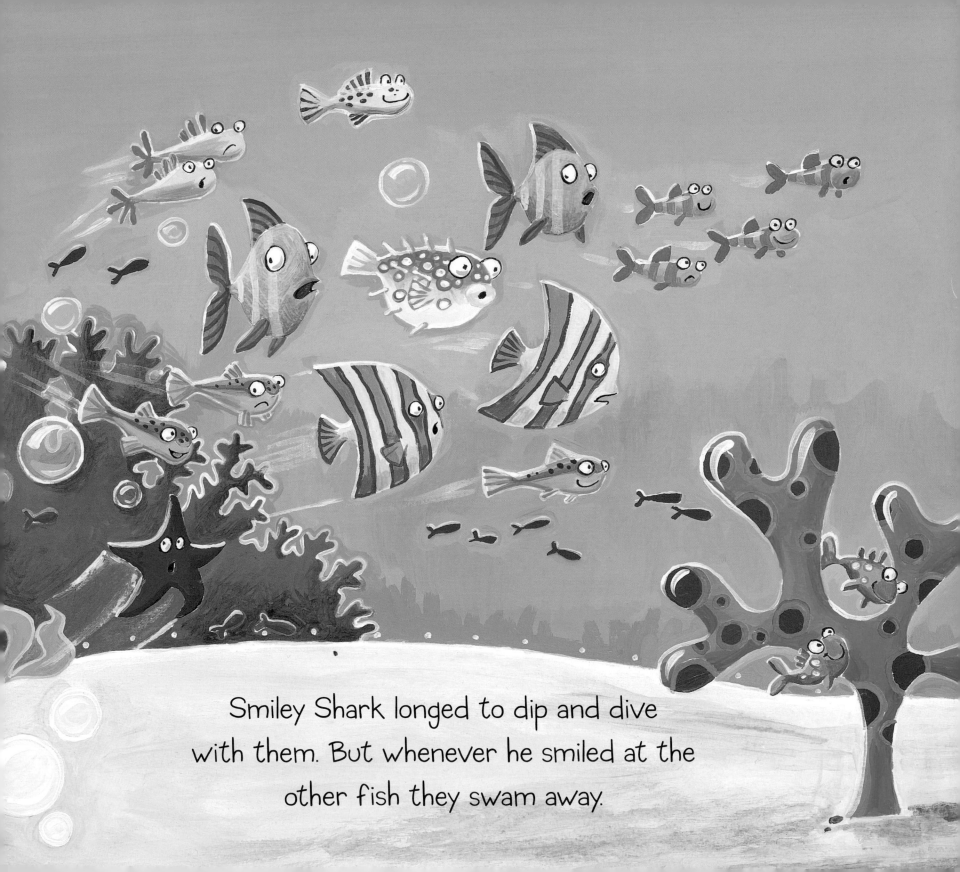

Smiley Shark longed to dip and dive
with them. But whenever he smiled at the
other fish they swam away.

"Will **YOU** play with me?"
he asked Angelfish.

Angelfish shivered and shook,
then raced away as fast as she could swim.

Starfish was twirling and whirling,
dancing and prancing.
"What fun!" giggled Smiley Shark.
But Starfish cartwheeled off across the
ocean floor as far away as she could go.

SWIRL!

Smiley Shark flashed his
grin at Jellyfish . . .

and Octopus . . .

and Catfish.

Off they swam,
as far from Smiley Shark
as they could get.

"Everyone is scared of my big white teeth," wailed Smiley Shark. He didn't feel much like smiling any more.

SPLISH! SPLASH!
Twisting and turning, splashing and churning,
the fish danced faster than ever. Smiley Shark
watched from a distance. But something was wrong.
The fish were swimming towards a . . .

...TRAP!

"Help!" cried the fish.
"Please help us, Smiley Shark!"

Smiley Shark swam round and
round the fisherman's net.
What could he do? How could he help?
The only thing Smiley Shark could do was . . .

"Hurrah!" cheered the fish.
"We're safe! Thank you, Smiley Shark!"

Now far away, in the deep rolling ocean,
Smiley Shark and his friends can be seen
dipping and diving, darting and dashing,
sploshing and splashing and

SMILING!

Dive into a book from Little Tiger Press

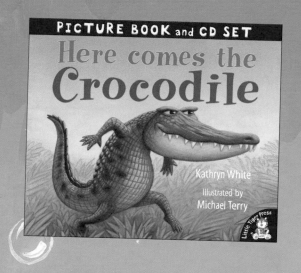

PICTURE BOOK and CD SET
Here comes the **Crocodile**
Kathryn White
Illustrated by Michael Terry

PICTURE BOOK and CD SET
The Very Lazy Ladybird
Isobel Finn & Jack Tickle

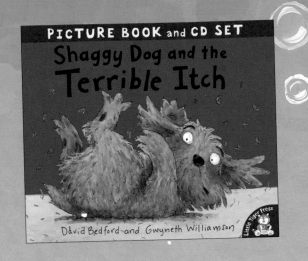

PICTURE BOOK and CD SET
Shaggy Dog and the **Terrible Itch**
David Bedford and Gwyneth Williamson

PICTURE BOOK and CD SET
The Crunching Munching Caterpillar
Sheridan Cain
Jack Tickle

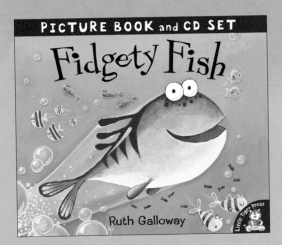

PICTURE BOOK and CD SET
Fidgety Fish
Ruth Galloway

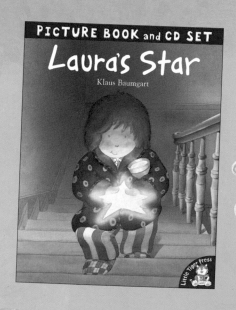

PICTURE BOOK and CD SET
Laura's Star
Klaus Baumgart

For information regarding any of the above
titles or for our catalogue, please contact us:
Little Tiger Press, 1 The Coda Centre,
189 Munster Road, London SW6 6AW, UK
Tel: 020 7385 6333 Fax: 020 7385 7333
E-mail: info@littletiger.co.uk www.littletigerpress.com